Bil Keane

FAWCETT GOLD MEDAL • NEW YORK

© Cowles Syndicate 1984, 1985

A Fawcett Gold Medal Book
Published by Ballantine Books
Copyright © 1989 by Bil Keane, Inc.
Distributed by King Features Syndicate, Inc.

All rights reserved under International and Pan-American Copyright Conventions, including the right to reproduce this book or portions thereof in any form. Published in the United States by Ballantine Books, a division of Random House, Inc., New York, and simultaneously in Canada by Random House of Canada Limited, Toronto.

Library of Congress Catalog Card Number: 89-91167

ISBN 0-449-13379-5

Manufactured in the United States of America

First Edition: August 1989
Third Printing: November 1990

"Don't bother Granddad. He's checkin'
his blood fresher."

"Mommy, do you know where Daddy
hid the nails?"

"Granddad has a cellulite phone in his car."

"If you open the back of the camera some of the dark will leak out!"

"Boy! You can really clap loud
with those things!"

"Whenever Mommy starts readin' this book
she calls somebody on the phone!"

"Dreams are when the Sandman lets you watch TV."

"When you grow up there won't be a
first female ANYTHING left for
you to be."

"Daddy, your face is drizzlin'."

"Your fishy KNOWS me, Grandma! He's
waggin' his tail!"

"Billy's 7; Jeffy's 2...no, Jeffy's 3;
Dolly's 4½...no, I think she's 5;
PJ's—let's see...."

"I'm like Rudolph. I went down
in history!"

"Call me if they show any
toy commercials!"

"We all hafta wash our hands so we can
sign Grandma's Christmas card."

"Aren't we gettin' one with lights?"

`'". . .While visions of NutraSweet plums danced in their heads."`

"Don't come in, Mommy! Don't come in!
You'll ruin Christmas!"

"...And if there's no snow then Santa
comes by bus."

"Would you donate something to our school's celebrity auction?"

"I'm allowed to ask for anything as long as it's assembled."

"Our TV set got pre-empted."

"Grandma's sendin' us a package by partial post."

"He's makin' a list and checkin'
his wife...."

"Why are we here again, Mommy? We were just here yesterday."

"Was the drummer boy the only little
kid invited to Baby Jesus'
birthday party?"

"Can we eat breakfast tonight so it won't get in the way tomorrow morning?"

"Wow! This was worth bein' good for!"

"STOP! I'LL CONFESS!"

"I got a new sled, but the snow wasn't included."

"Don't bring PJ out to show him off.
Everyone here either has a baby—
or hasn't."

"That's what they pour over everybody's
head when they win a big game."

"Mommy says we can have midnight at
9 o'clock!"

"They took the Christmas tree."

"Come on, needle. Say 'ahh.'"

"I bet that tree wishes it was growin'
in Florida."

"I'm here in the u-tiddly room!"

"Can't we teach PJ to sit and stay so
he'll quit followin' me?"

"There wasn't enough snow for a whole snowman, so we just made a bust."

"PJ's lucky. He's just the size of a hug."

"We're gonna see the President's
inoculation!"

"Daddy says if a girl wants to grow up to be president she should start by keepin' her room clean and brushin' her teeth."

"Instead of letting Daddy settle this couldn't
we let Judge Wapner do it?"

"Jimmy! What does that mean?"

"I think it means 'the car won't start.'"

"Morrie's mom went back to school and
nobody MADE her!"

"Mommy, will you see if Daddy got
my homework right?"

"February is when the groundhog puts
valentines in the cherry trees."

"Daddy! They only gave you
11 doughnuts!"

"Birds like to make asterisks."

"Kittycat's doin' her imitation of
a camel."

"Jeffy's playin' a song on the
push-button phone!"

"Well, yes — we'll see Granddad someday when we go to heaven."

"Could I just wait in the car?"

"They all sounded OK till 'clean'."

"Daddy's bakin' a cake. He said so."

"Mmm! Could I wear some of that
'nilla for perfume?"

"You corrected my English so much I
forgot what I was goin' to say!"

"You steer by pulling its ears."

"Oh no! He brought flowers 'stead
of candy!"

"Who marked up the ceiling?"
"Not me." "Not me."

"Grandma said she was in the pink, but
she's wearin' yellow!"

"Which one comes sooner — 'later' or
'afterwhile?' "

"Would you iron this a little, Mommy? It's my homework!"

"Look! I know how to make an
excitement mark!"

"This place behind your knee is your
knee pit."

"Before you come in here, Mommy — you love me, right?"

"There, Daddy! PJ's showing you how to
do it."

"I wish I was a latchkey kid!"

"It's OK if they hafta pull your tooth, Grandma. Your second one will grow in in no time!"

"It's a ruler. It's for spanking and sometimes for measurin'."

"I bet Larry Bird's mother let HIM
dribble in the house!"

"Balloons fly like they're in a
slow motion replay!"

"Oooo-oooo! I know! I know that one!
Can I answer? Oooo-oooo!..."

"Mommy, why do some of your shoes have legs on them?"

"Revolving doors work magic. They turn
crowds into regular people!"

"Grandma says she's feelin' fit as
a fizzle!"

"We hafta wait for an empty place
to come by."

"HALT!"

"Go ahead. Make my day."

"Grandma likes to travel by train 'cause
their landing gears are always down."

"That's your birth certificate. They
give you that for bein' born."

"Wouldn't it be neat if Bill Cosby was
our father? He's FUNNY!"

"Frankly, Shirley, I see nothing wrong
with your loving a younger man."

"Does St. Patrick bring us stuff on
his day like Santa Claus does?"

"You better stop that, Jeffy! Mommy
can see you in her little mirror."

"Mommy, when you wash grapes how much soap do you use?"

"Are the clean towels in the closet
or the dryer?"

"Mommy says the only smokin' they should
allow is the peace pipe."

"Don't we have any cat food that's
mouse-flavored?"

"If it says 'FREE INSIDE,' that's the
one we like."

"Babies sure are a cute way to
start people!"

"Look! NOBODY'S going to New York with Daddy. It's a BUSINESS trip!"

"We just saw the plane Daddy's takin' to New York! I saw him WAVIN' to us!"

"If you want me to I'll SNORE like
Daddy so you won't be lonely,
Mommy!"

"Mommy's outside, Daddy. How's the
weather there? Jeffy wants to talk
to you. Wanna hear a joke?. . . All
right, Daddy, I'll get her!"

"Will God accept a long-distance
prayer for somebody who's
visiting New York?"

"... And you're helping Mommy, Jeffy?
Good boy! Yes ... Yes ... Yes ... OK,
put PJ on, but quickly! ..."

"I get to sit in Daddy's place tomorrow
night 'cause GIRLS can be the man of
the family, too! Can't they,
Mommy?"

"Daddy! Daddy! Did you bring
us anything?"

"Wow! An airlines magazine for me, tiny soaps for Dolly, a bag of peanuts for Jeffy, and stirrers for PJ! Thank you, Daddy!"

"You guys hafta sleep down here tonight
so you don't scare the Easter
Bunny away!"

"Those are things the kids found during
their Easter egg hunt."

"Whenever I can't wait till tomorrow all of a sudden it's yesterday!"

"April fool!"

"Same here. Egg salad again!"

"We'll be there shortly!"
"Oh, good! I was afraid you'd say we'd
be there longly."

"There are millions of poor cats all over the world who'd love to have that food!"

"That's not the way to hold a Frisbee!"

"If you sneak a piece of peppermint candy
don't breathe near Mommy!"

"I'll dance with your bottom half."

"When will it be 'later,' Mommy? Claire's
mother said to come back later."

"I think I'll take a rain check on
school today."

"Then the caterpillar puts on his butterfly
costume and flies away."

"Did God write the Bible with a word processor, a typewriter, or just a feather and ink?"

"Guess what? I can count all the way up
to the very highest number!"

"Next time you drop a can of soda,
wait a few minutes before
opening it."

"I wish Grandma had a toll-free number."

"PJ doesn't know how to button or
tie yet, but he can Velcro."

"You hafta listen to me with your eyes, Daddy. Not just your ears."

"Why are your fingers dancin' to the music?"

"Know why God hasta take some old
people? They used up all their
birthdays."

"Most of my M&M's have W's on them."

"Dolly learned to skate quite quickly."
"Yes, it only took about 10 sittings."

"Brian is very handsome — 'specially
when he smiles and the sun shines
on his braces."

"Will I hafta start every day by putting on my clothes for the rest of my life?"

You can have lots more fun
with
BIL KEANE and
THE FAMILY CIRCUS

Buy these books at your local bookstore or use this handy coupon for ordering:

_____THE FAMILY CIRCUS	12823	3.50
_____ANY CHILDREN?	12800	2.95
_____GOOD MORNING, SUNSHINE!	12895	2.95
_____GO TO YOUR ROOM!	12610	2.95
_____GRANDMA WAS HERE!	12835	3.50
_____HELLO, GRANDMA?	12930	2.95
_____MY TURN NEXT!	12792	2.95
_____PEEKABOO, I LOVE YOU!	12824	2.95
_____PICK UP WHAT THINGS?	12785	3.50

FAWCETT MAIL SALES
Dept. TA 201 E. 50th St., New York, N.Y. 10022

Please send me the FAWCETT BOOKS I have checked above. I am enclosing $.............(add $2.00 to cover postage and handling for the first book and 50¢ each additional book). Send check or money order—no cash or C.O.D.'s please. Prices are subject to change without notice. Valid in U.S. only. All orders are subject to availability of books.

Name_____

Address_____

City_____State_____Zip Code_____
30   Allow at least 4 weeks for delivery.   1/91   TA-60